USBORNE
100 PTEROSAURS
TO FOLD AND FLY

Illustrated by Sarah Allen
and David Sossella

Designed by Poppy Pearce
and Brian Voakes

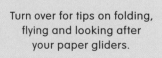

Turn over for tips on folding,
flying and looking after
your paper gliders.

Useful tips

Here are some helpful tips that will make your gliders fly more effectively and keep them in good condition.

How to launch your paper glider

Follow these steps for a perfect take-off and landing:

- Stand facing forward.

- Hold each glider just in front of the middle of its body.

- Pull back and then throw forward in a long, smooth movement to release your glider.

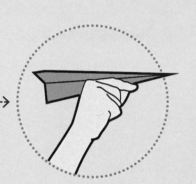

Folding

- Place a ruler along the folds and press down to keep them sharp.

- If you want to keep your glider for another day, store it flat inside a book.

- If your glider gets wet, or won't fly... fold a new one!

Flying

- Try changing the angle of your glider's wing to alter its flight.

Wings up

Wings down

Add a wing tip fold

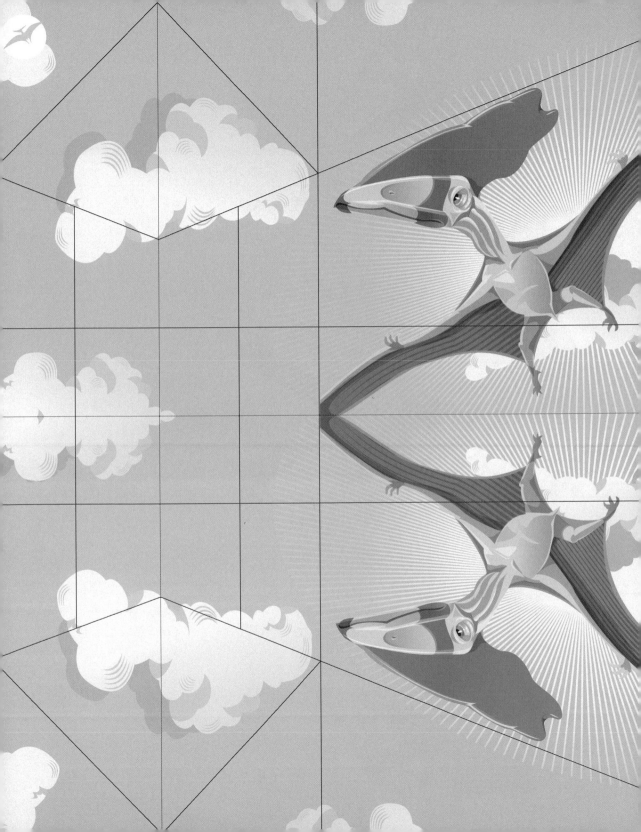

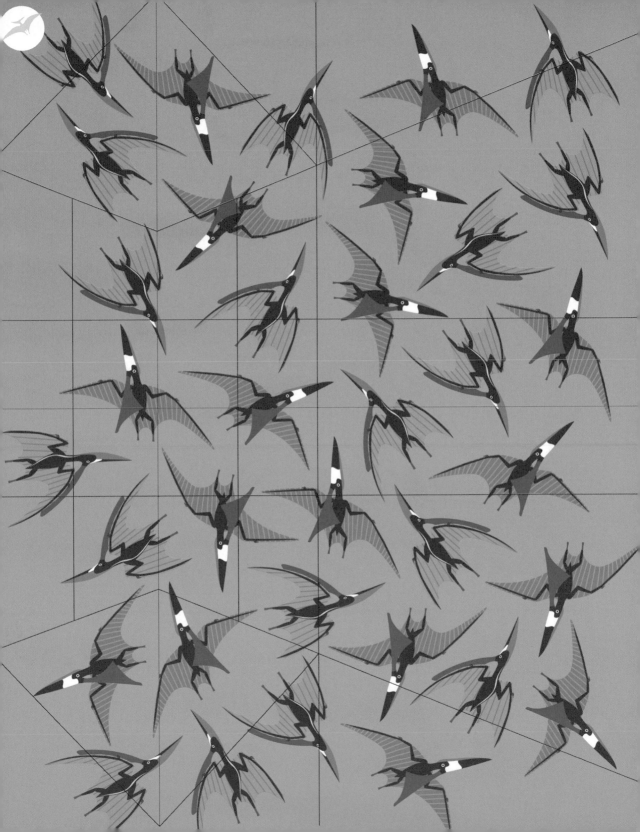

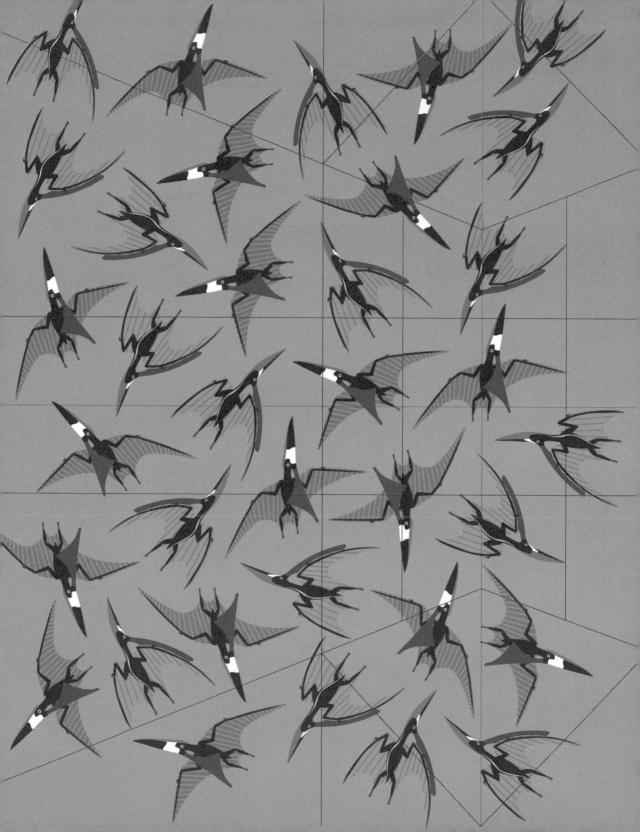

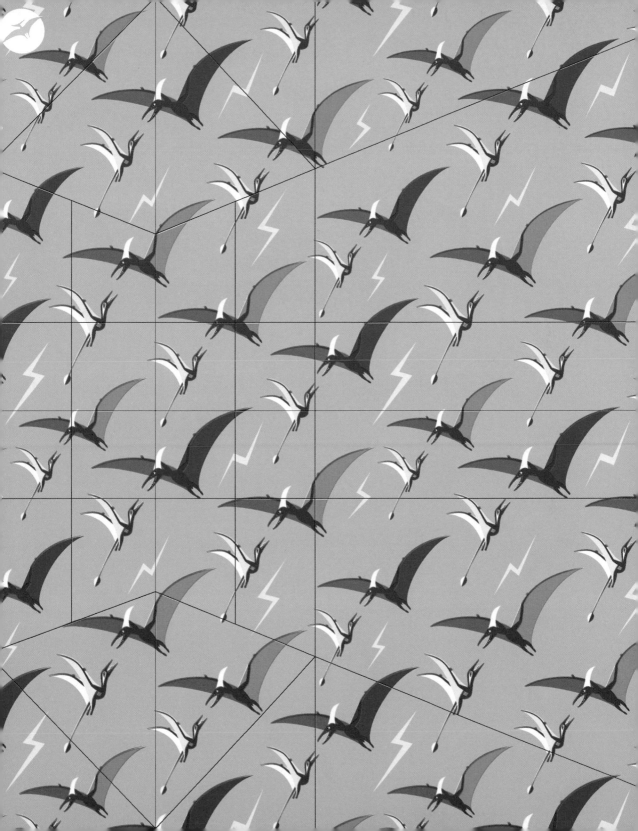

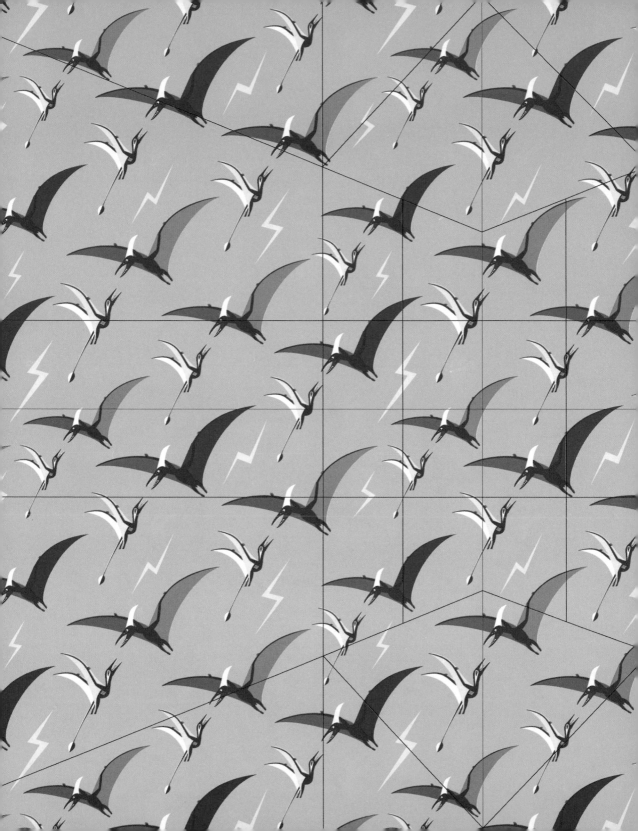

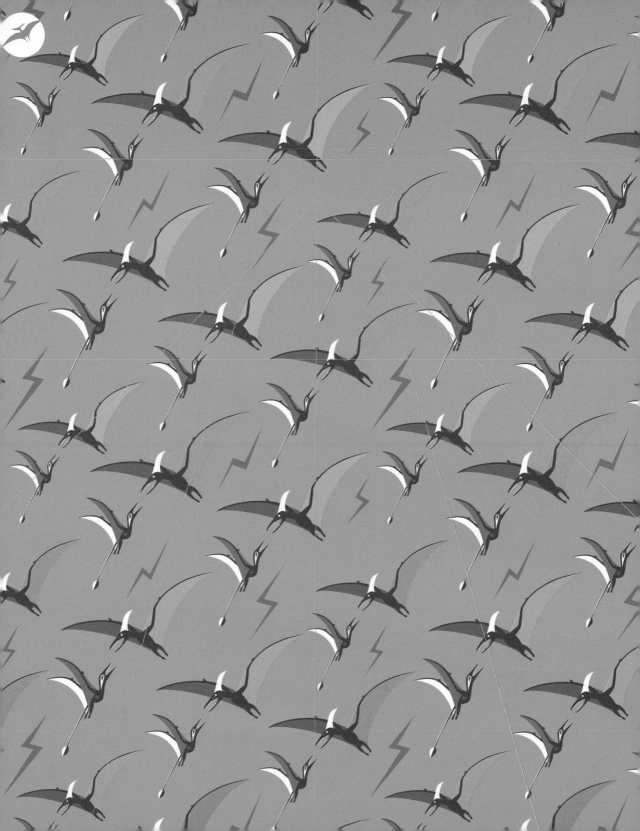

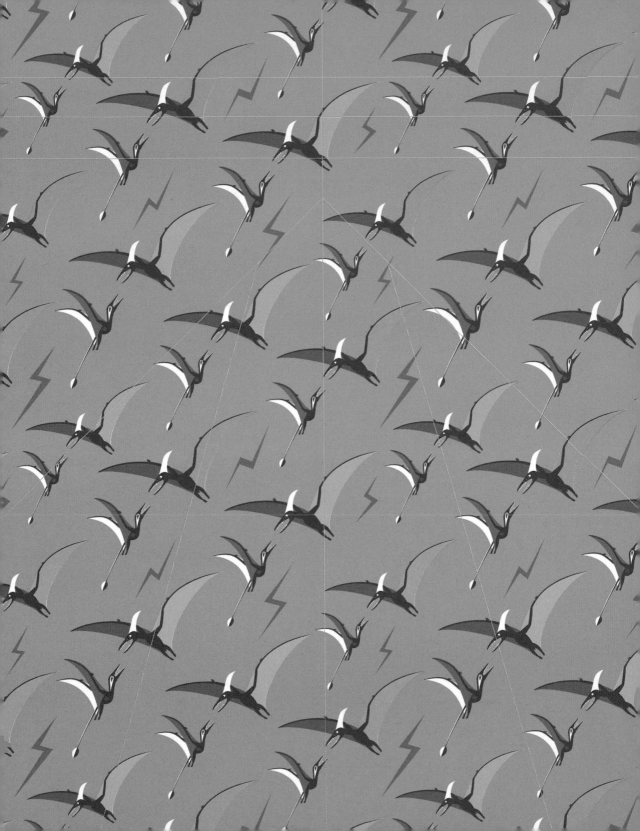

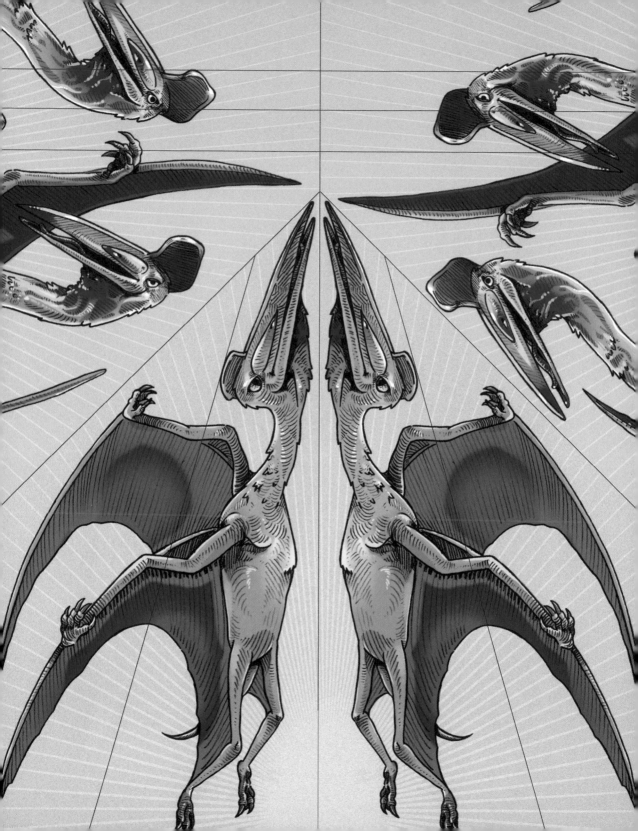

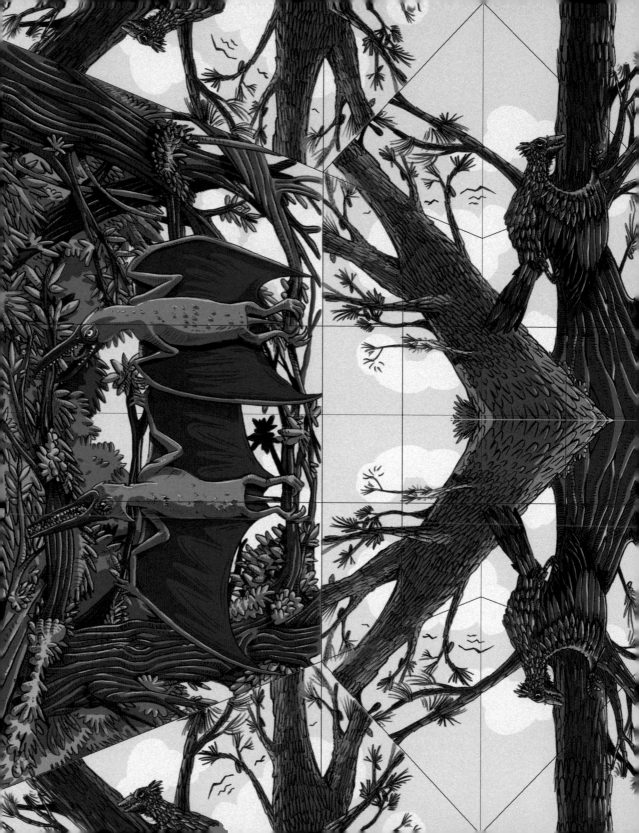

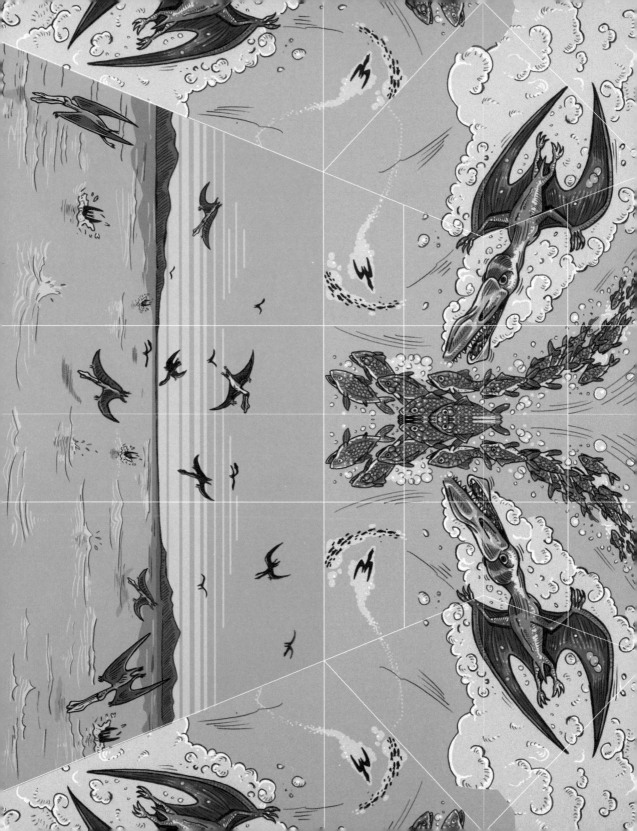

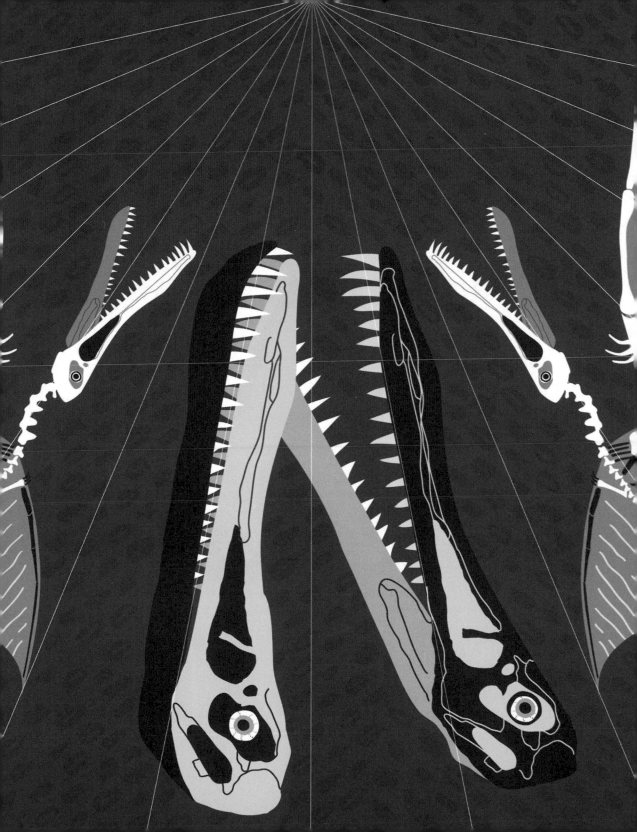

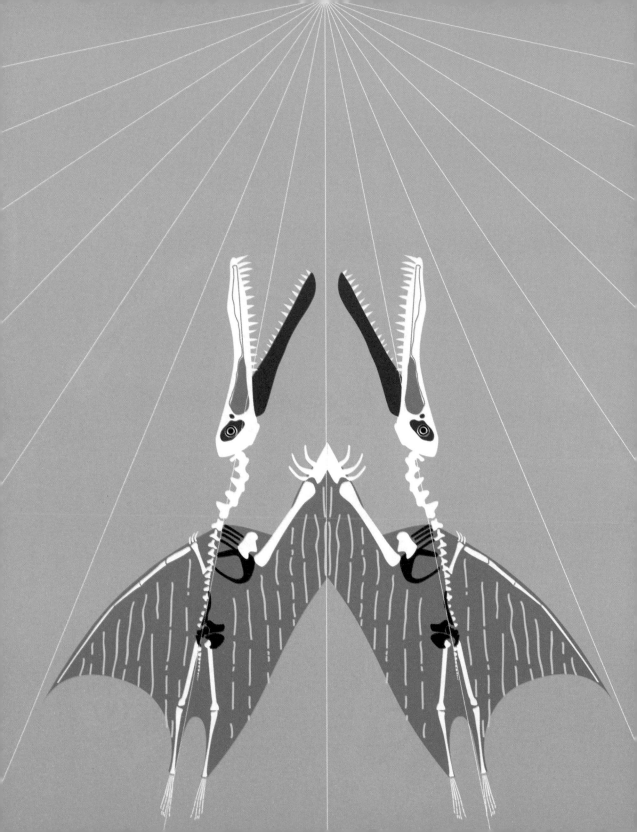

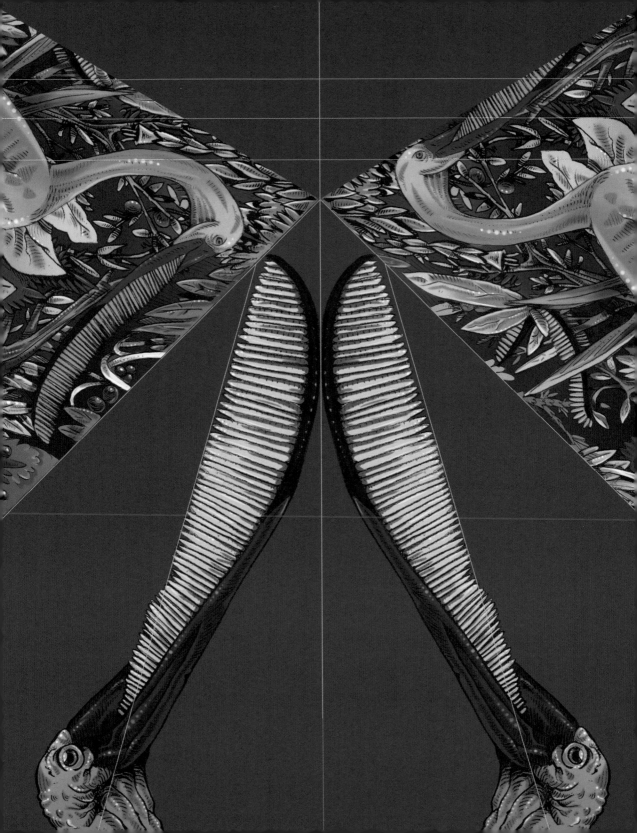

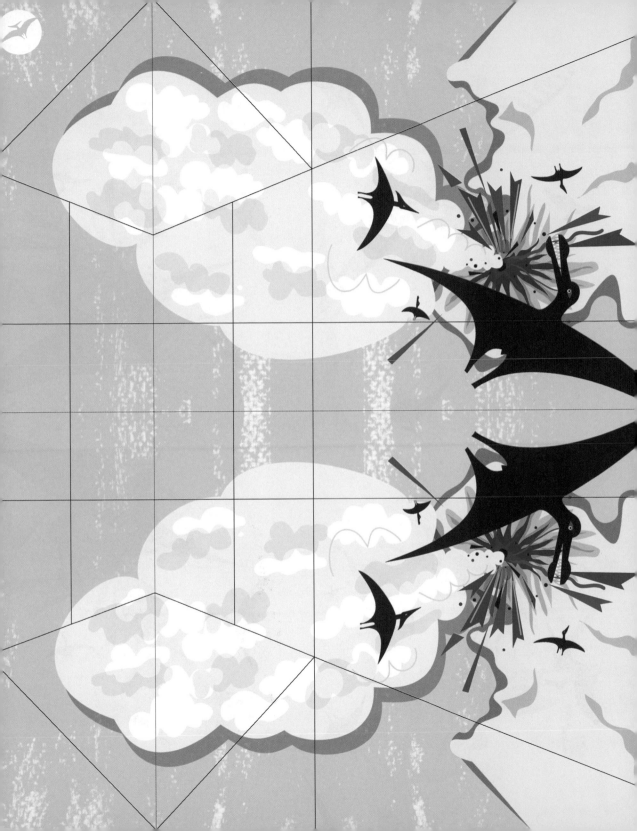

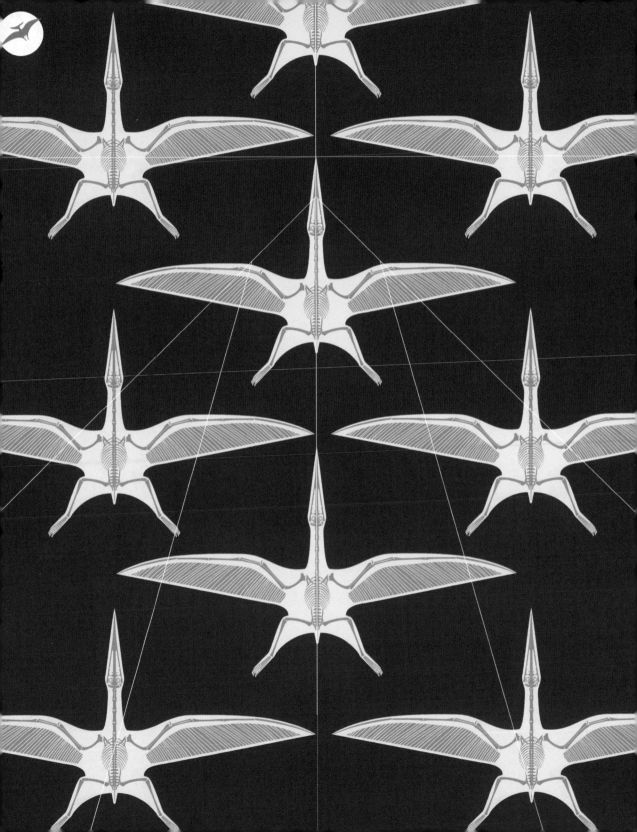

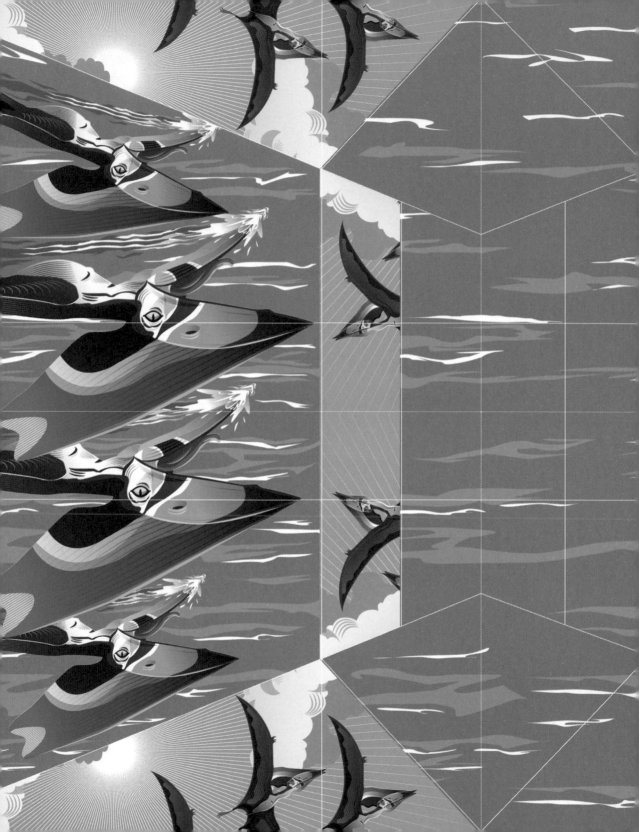

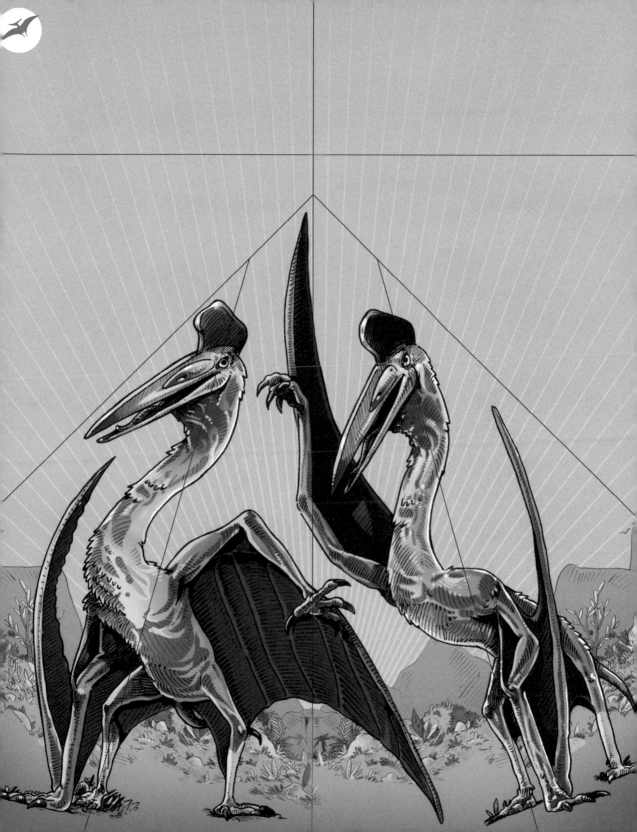

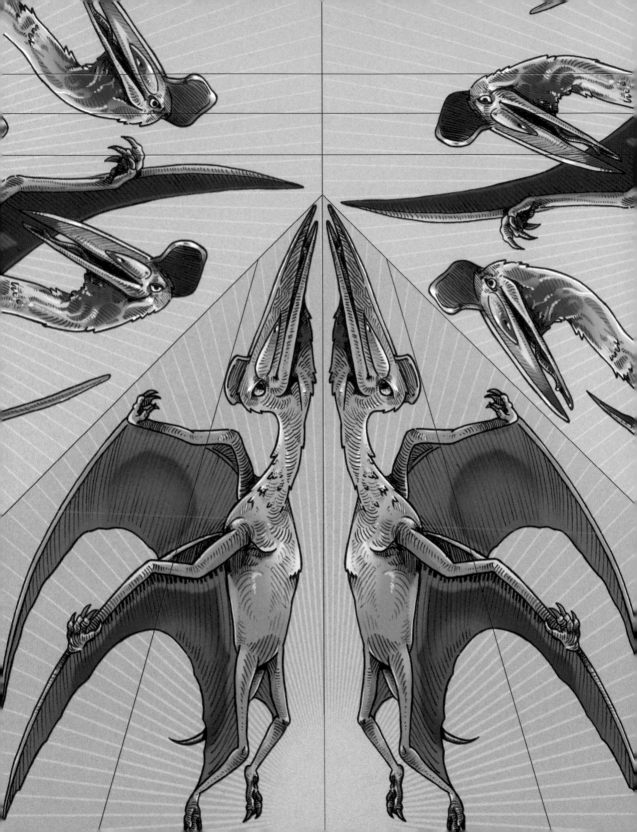

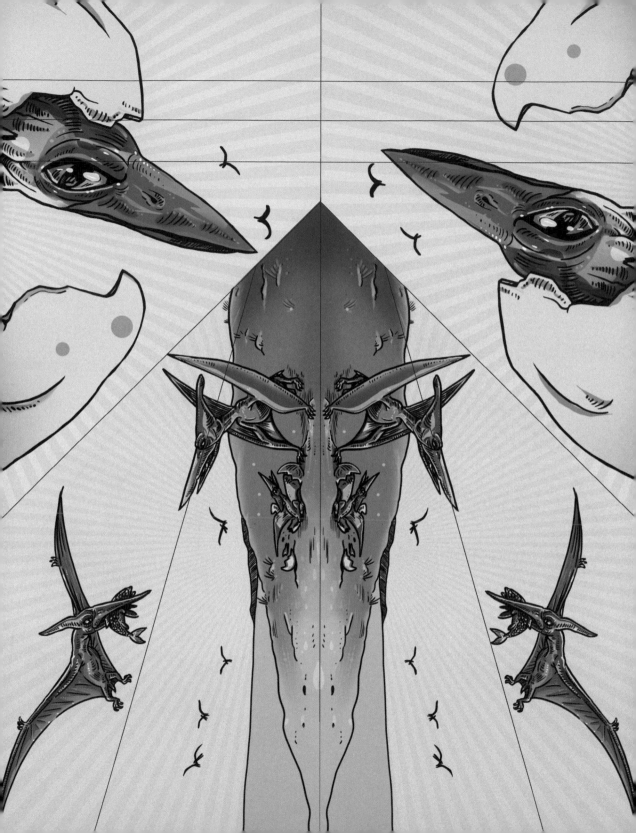

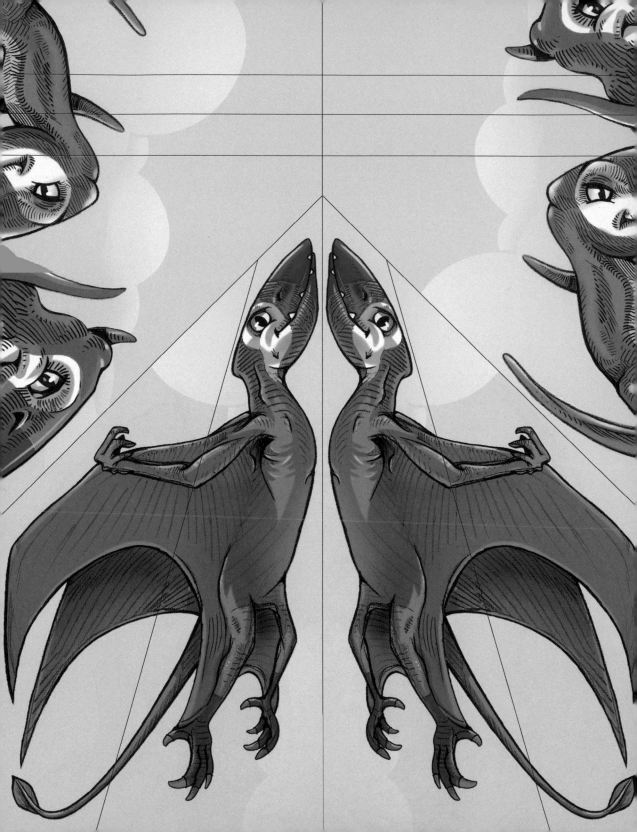

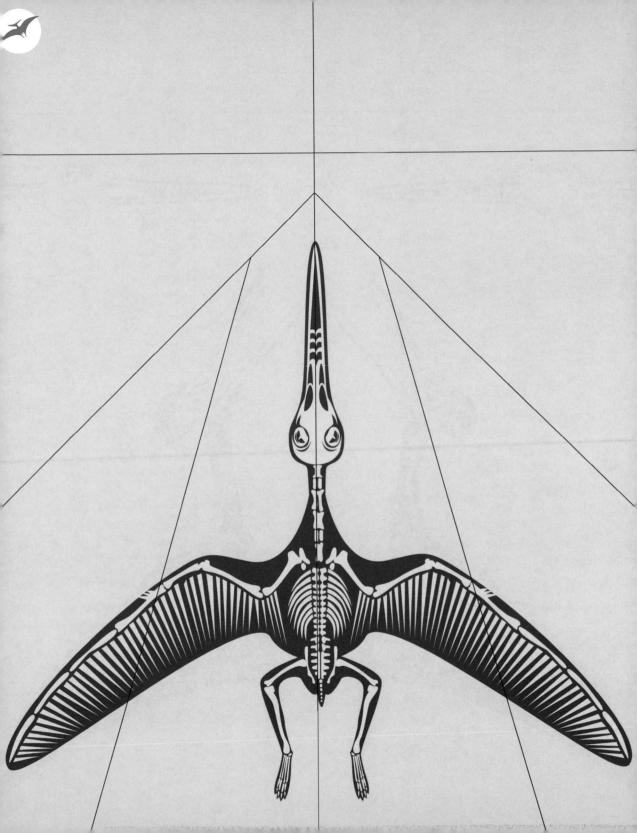

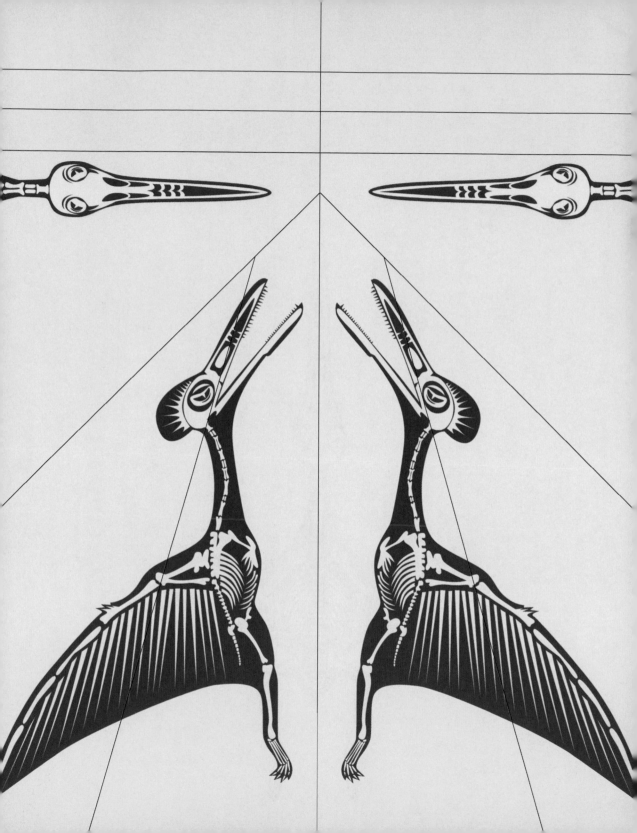

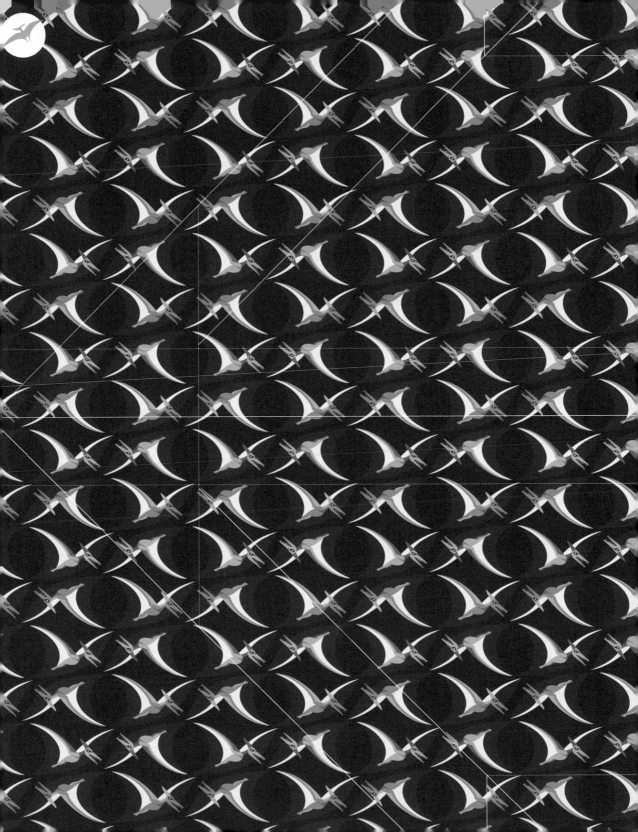

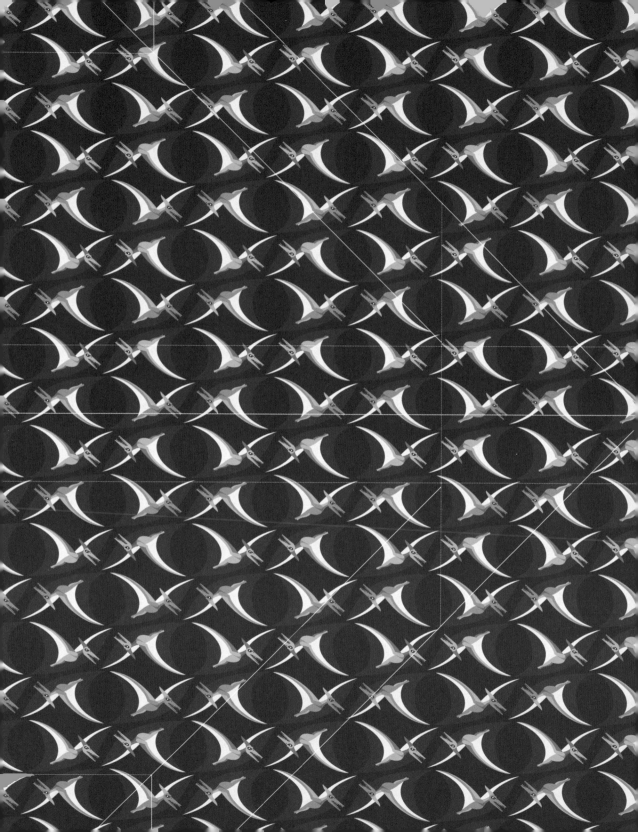

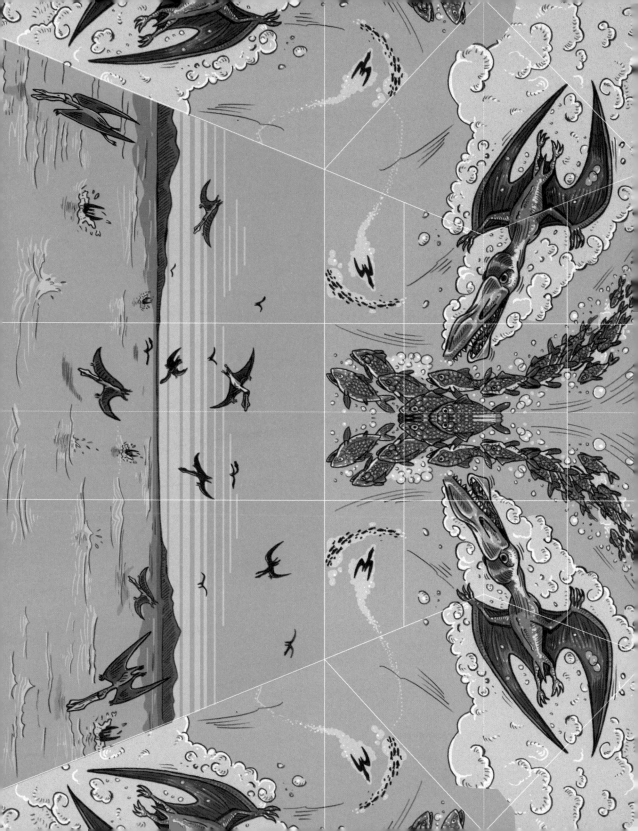

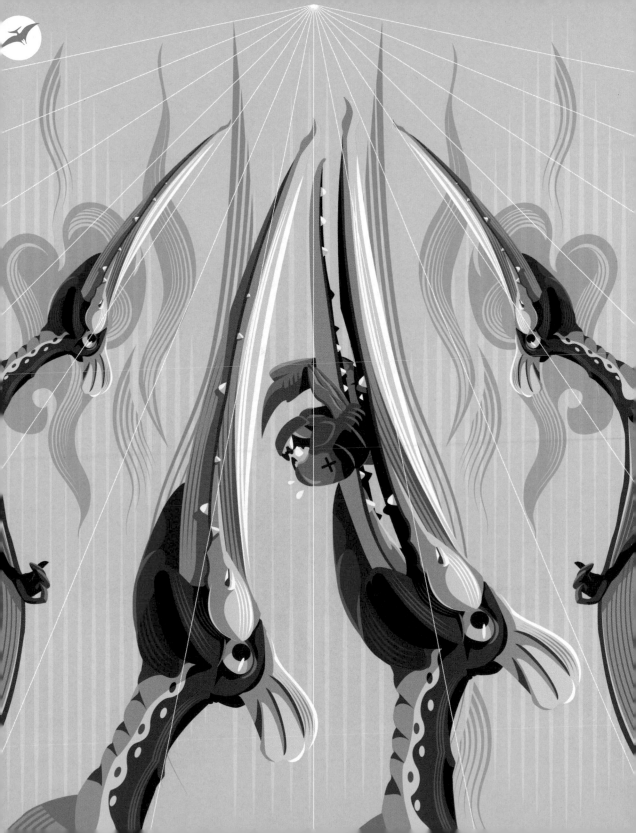

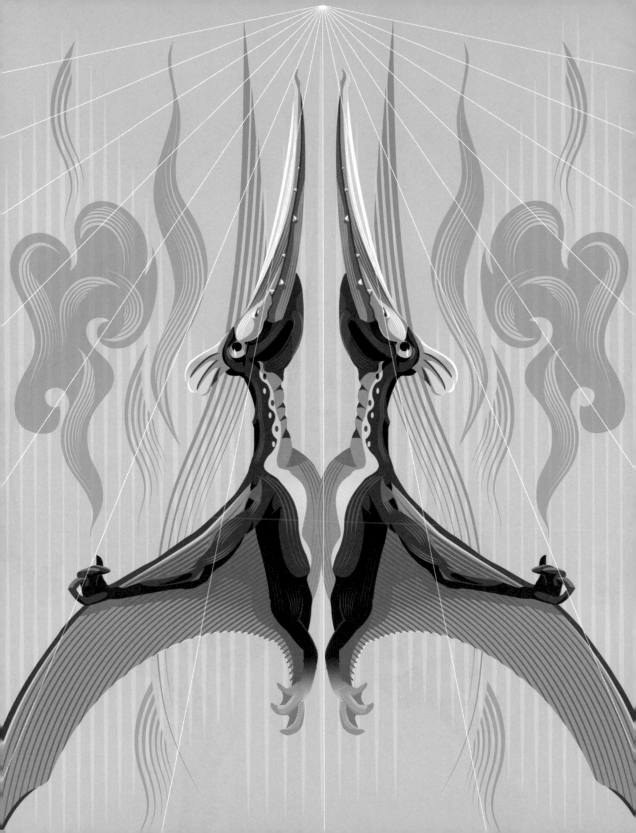

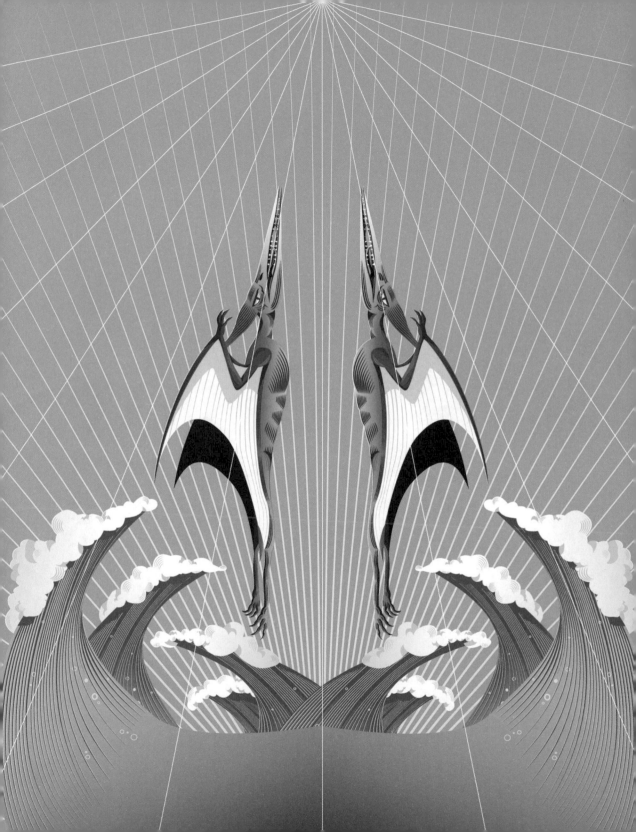

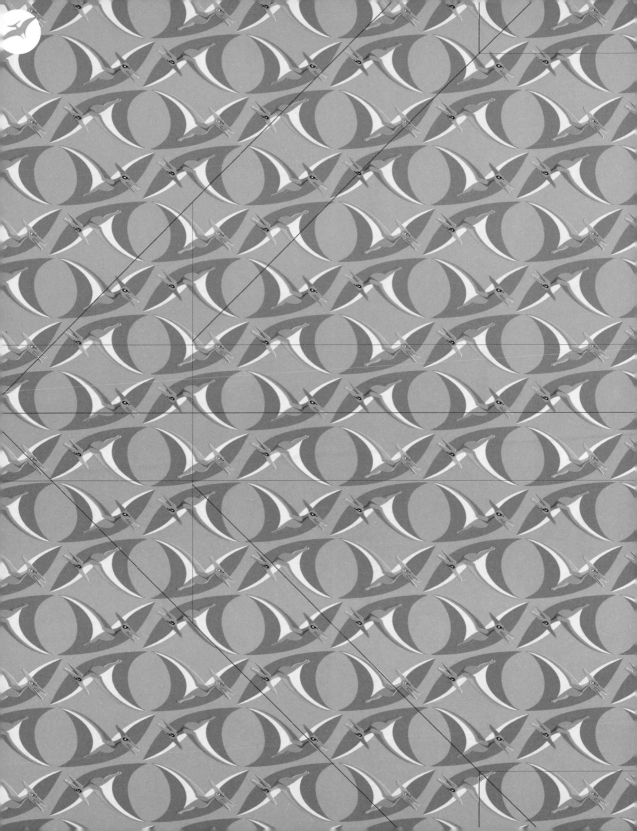

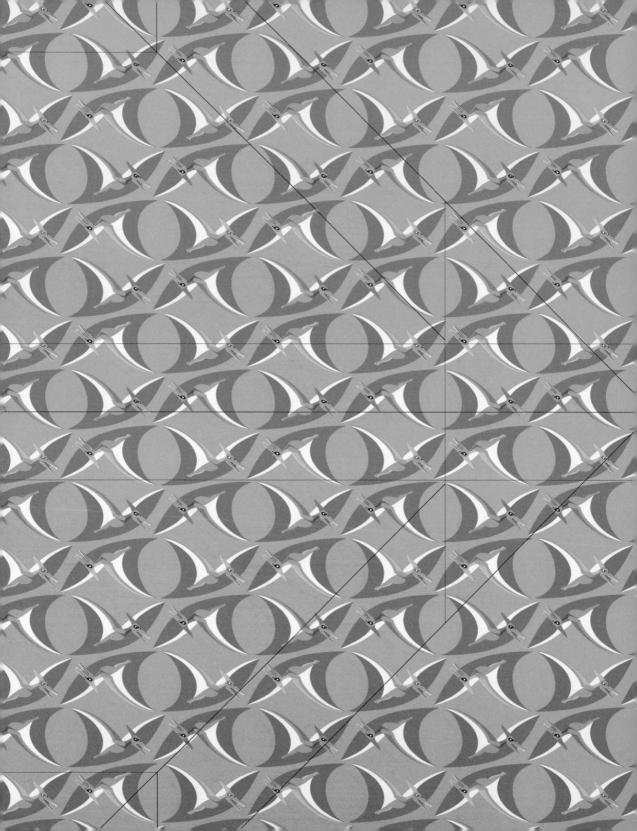

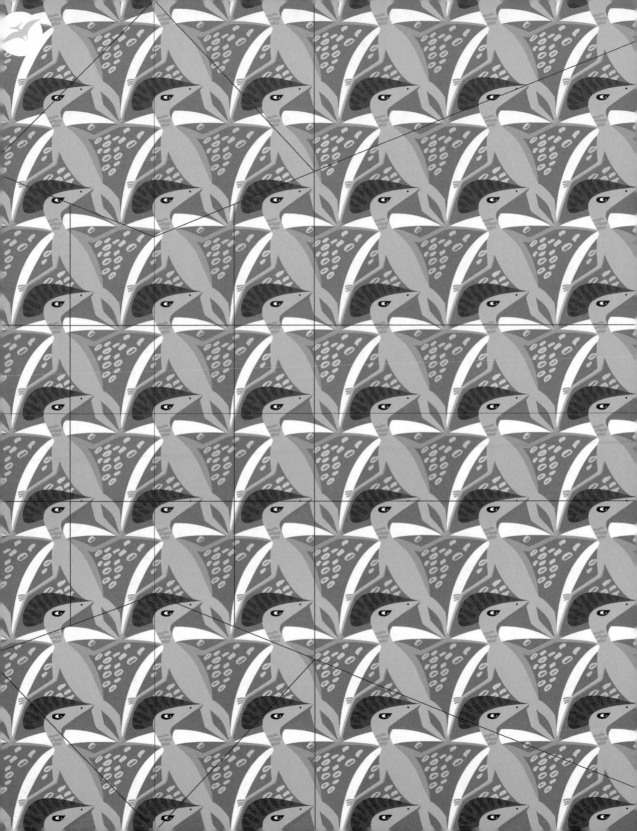

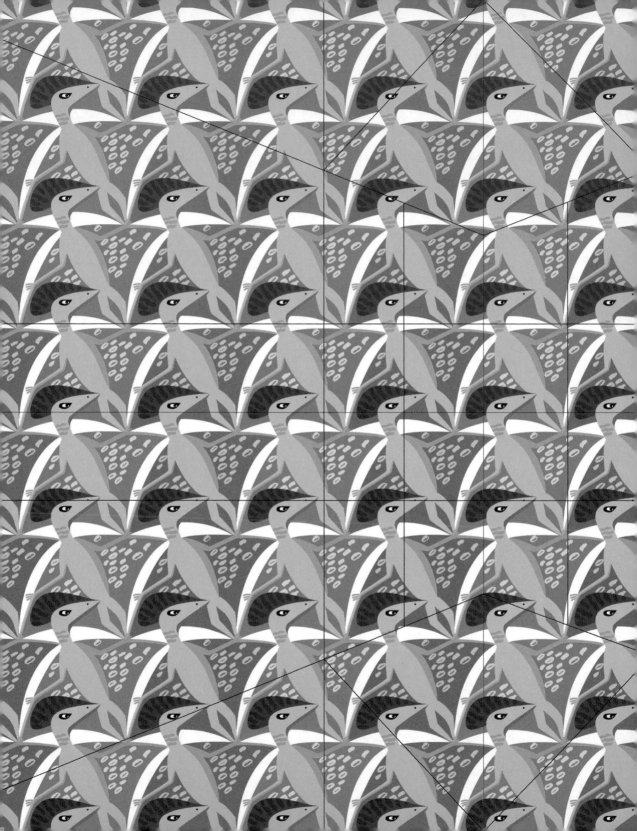

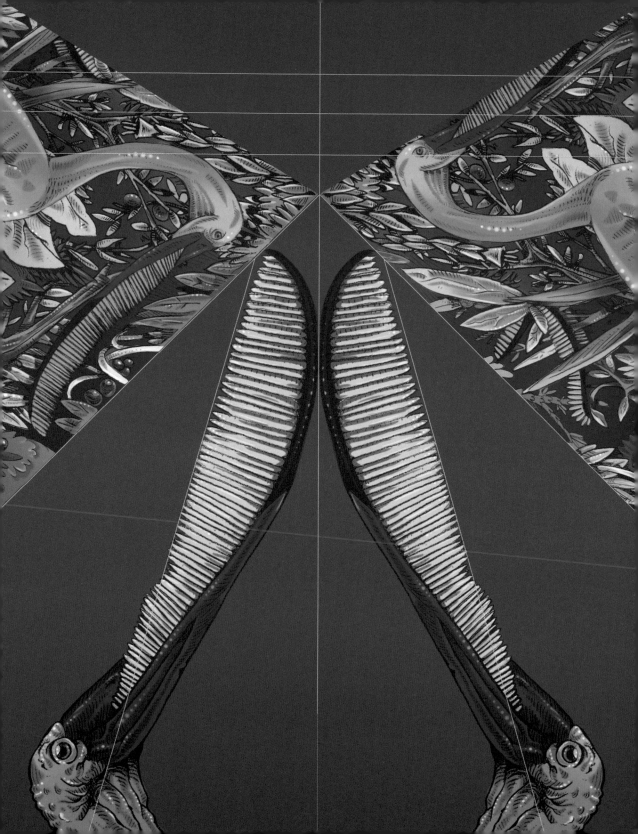

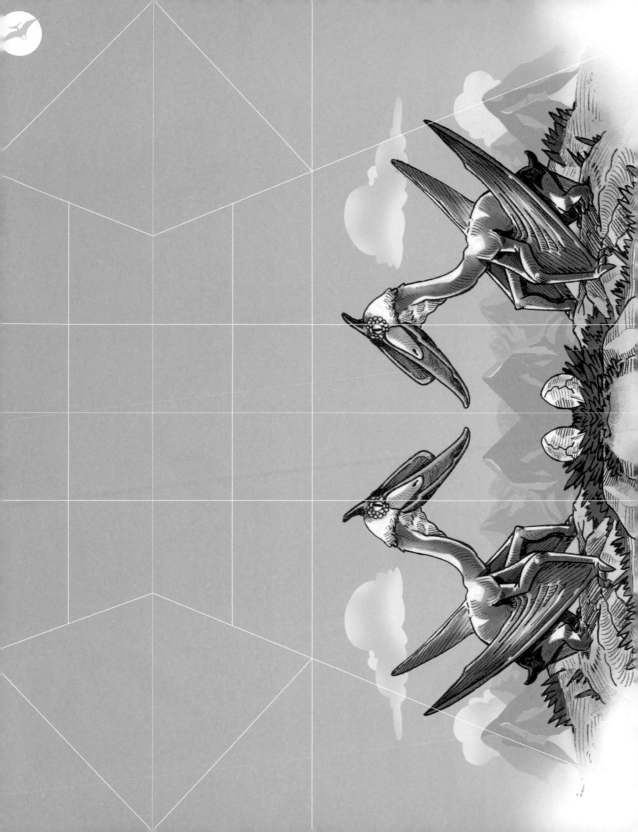

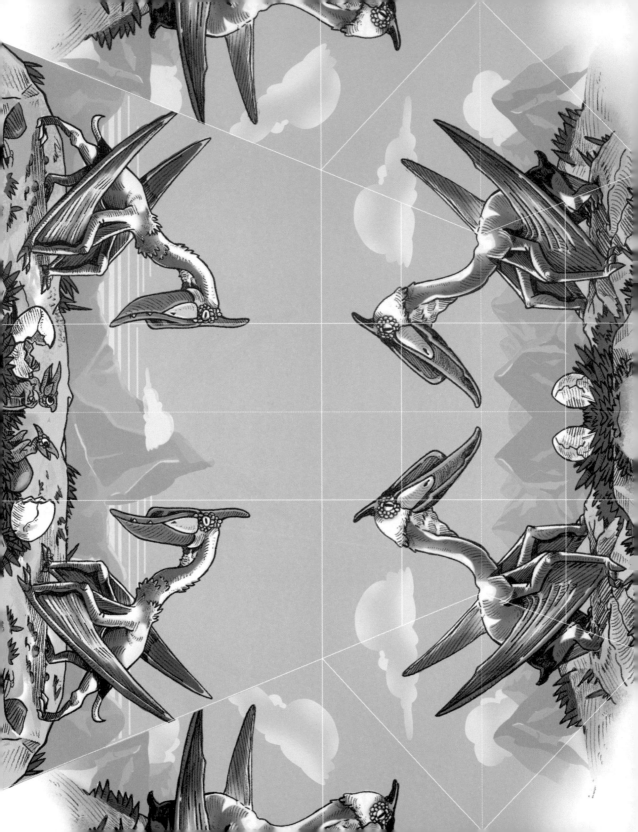

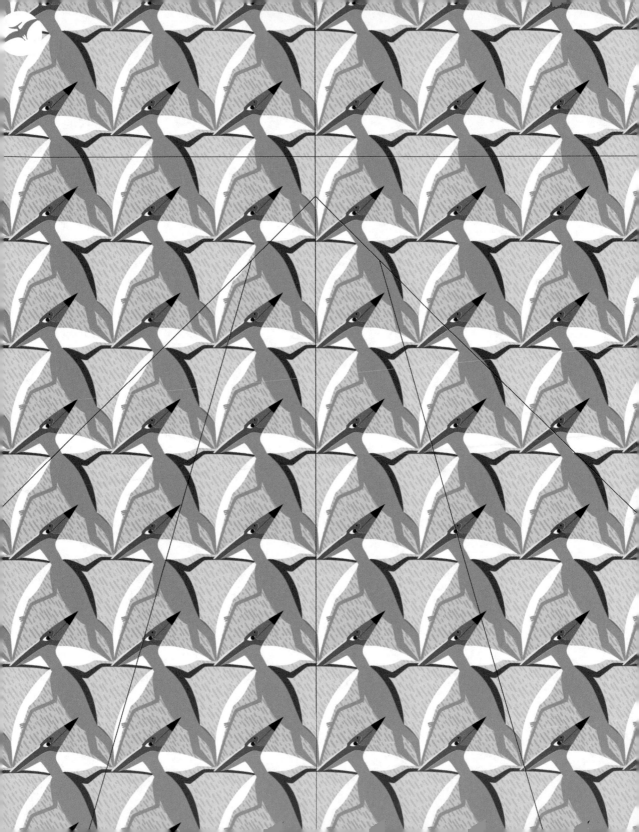

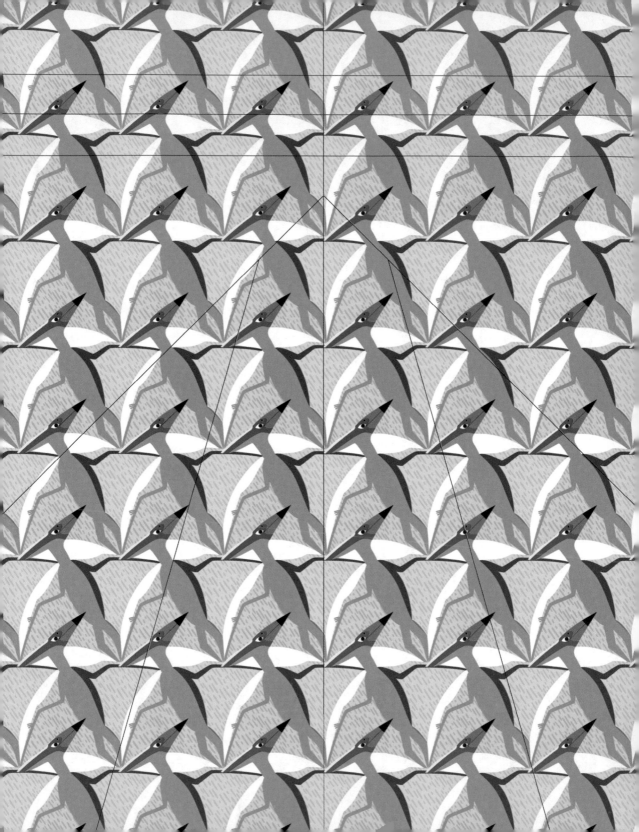

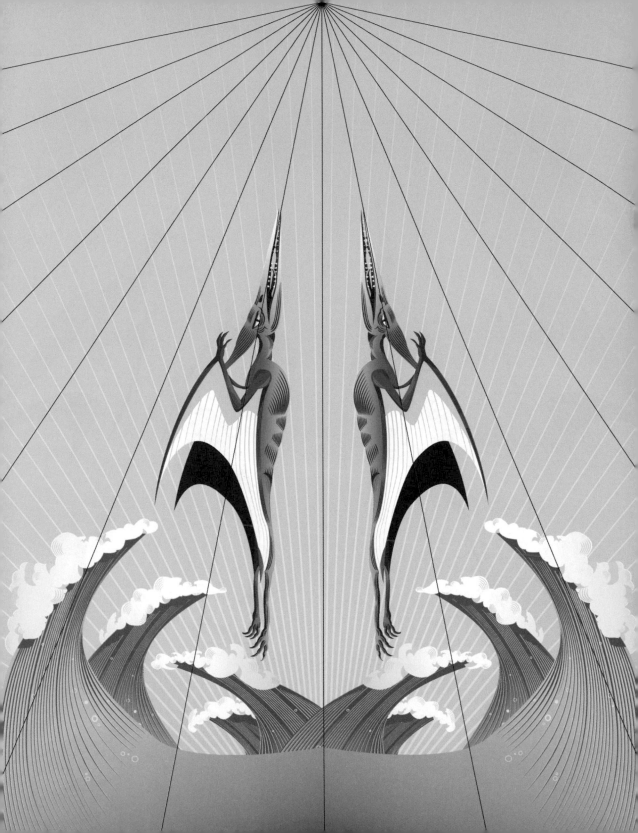

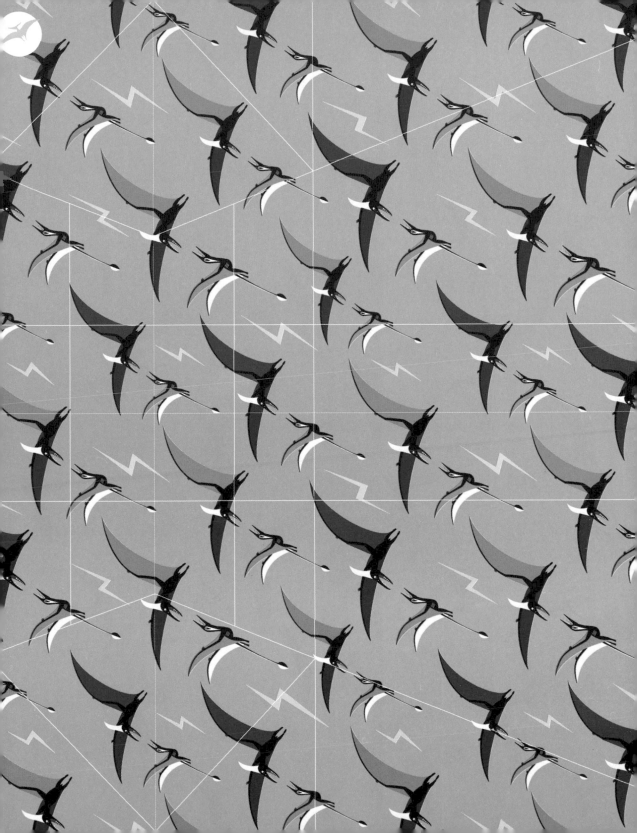

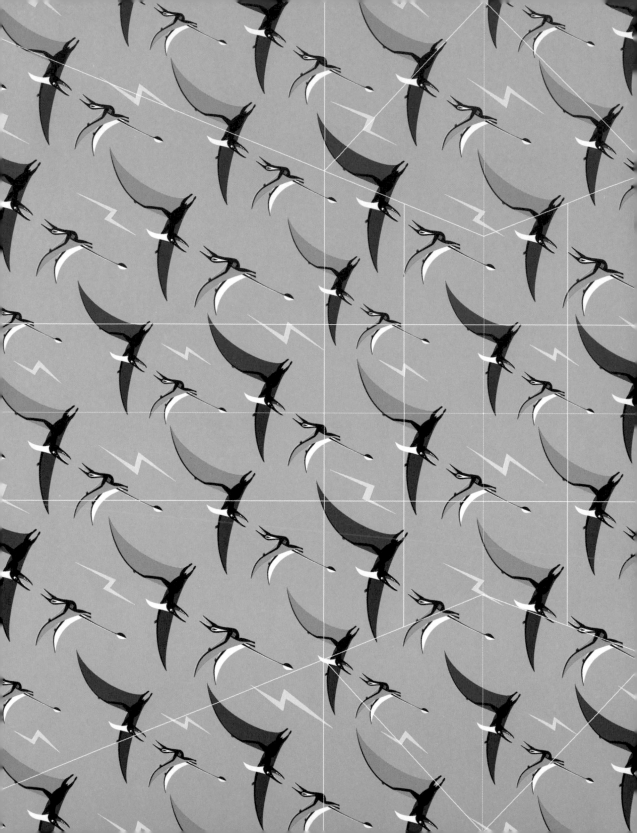

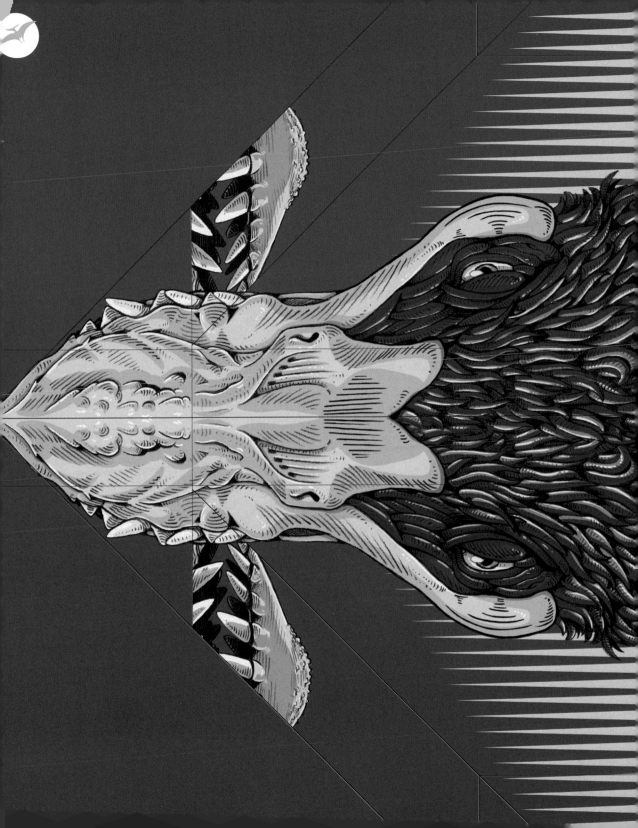